Hot Wheels

by Grace Hansen

abdobooks.com

Published by Abdo Kids, a division of ABDO, P.O. Box 398166, Minneapolis, Minnesota 55439.
Copyright © 2023 by Abdo Consulting Group, Inc. International copyrights reserved in all countries.
No part of this book may be reproduced in any form without written permission from the publisher.
Abdo Kids Jumbo™ is a trademark and logo of Abdo Kids.

Printed in China.

102022

012023

Photo Credits: Alamy, AP Images, Getty Images, Shutterstock,
©JeromeG111 p1/ CC BY-NC-ND 2.0, ©Joe Haupt p.6,7/ CC BY-SA 2.0

Production Contributors: Teddy Borth, Jennie Forsberg, Grace Hansen
Design Contributors: Candice Keimig, Pakou Moua

Library of Congress Control Number: 2022937180

Publisher's Cataloging-in-Publication Data

Names: Hansen, Grace, author.

Title: Hot Wheels / by Grace Hansen

Description: Minneapolis, Minnesota : Abdo Kids, 2023 | Series: Toy mania! | Includes online resources and
    index.

Identifiers: ISBN 9781098264277 (lib. bdg.) | ISBN 9781098264833 (ebook) | ISBN 9781098265113
    (Read-to-Me ebook)

Subjects: LCSH: Hot Wheels toys--Juvenile literature. | Toy automobiles--Juvenile literature. | Toys--
    Juvenile literature. | Mattel, Inc.--Juvenile literature.

Classification: DDC 629.221--dc23

Table of Contents

Hot Wheels

Hot Wheels came racing onto the scene in 1968. The shiny toy cars haven't lost their **luster** since. They have been popular with kids and collectors alike for decades.

Fast Track to Success

In 1945, Elliot Handler, his wife Ruth, and Harold Matson **founded** Mattel Creations. At first, the company sold wooden picture frames. Doll furniture was built with the leftover wood. Soon, Mattel focused only on toys.

TWIRL
TUNE
PLAYS REAL MUSIC
PLAYS REAL MUSIC
TWIRL-A-TUNE
COPYRIGHT 1951 MATTEL INCORPORATED • LOS ANGELES, CALIF. • PATENT NOS. 2,504,646 - 2,504,452   MADE IN U.S.A.
STOCK NO. 442

The Handlers came up with many popular toys. Barbie, **debuting** in 1959, was one of their brightest ideas. But the couple didn't stop there.

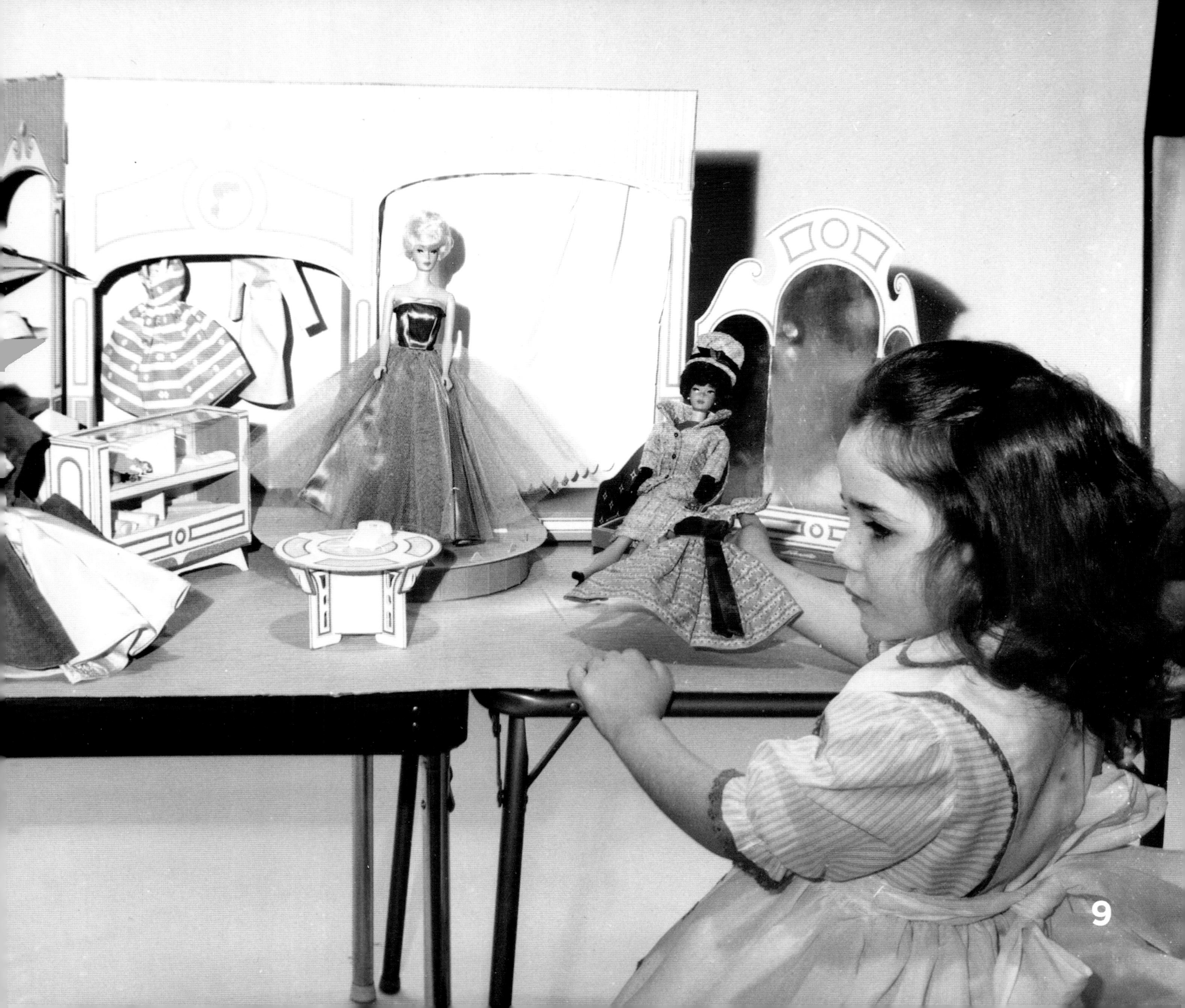

Small **die-cast** cars were already toys that were loved by kids. But Elliot wanted to make a better option. And that meant cooler and faster toy cars!

11

Elliot hired Harry Bradley.
Harry designed automobiles
for General Motors. He helped
build the perfect miniature
car. Elliot made sure the cars
looked **striking**. **Prototypes**
were painted white to check for
imperfections.

Hot Wheels
Custom Camaro
prototype

The tiny cars were tested in the factory. Workers made sure each one could move at least 50 feet (15 m) without stopping. Then the cars were placed in clear packaging. This would allow kids to see which car they were buying.

Hot Wheels
9/10
50 GRAND PRIX
LAMBORGHINI COUNTACH PACE CAR
HW EXOTICS
3+
hotwheels.com
momo
DODGE CHALLENGER DRIFT CAR
PORSCHE 935
'98 Honda Prelude
HW FERR
NISSAN SKYLINE 2000 GT-R
PONTIAC FIREBIRD
HW FLAMES
THEN AND NOW
Hot Wheels
CHEVY BEL AIR
8/10
HW RACE DAY
NISSAN

The Sweet Sixteen

On May 18, 1968, Mattel released the Custom Camaro. It was part of the Hot Wheels line known as the Sweet Sixteen. The other 15 cars came soon after. In the first year, more than 16 million of them zoomed off the shelves!

FORD J-CAR
CALIFORNIA CUSTOM STYLING
SPECTRAFLAME PAINT JOBS
MAG WHEELS RED STRIPED SLICKS
OPENING HOODS
CUSTOM CORVETTE
CUSTOM BARRACUDA
CUSTOM FIREBIRD
CUSTOM COUGAR
CUSTOM CAMARO
CUSTOM ELDORADO
CUSTOM T-BIRD
CUSTOM Volkswagen
CUSTOM MUSTANG
HOT HEAP
SILHOUETTE
THE ONE AND ONLY MATTEL HOT WHEELS CARS.
RALLY CASES
'Mag' wheel holds 12 or 24 HOT WHEELS. Only for collectors. Only by Mattel.
4 HOT WHEELS SUPER-CHARGER SETS
You get SUPER-CHARGER, cars, track, all the goodies you need. Choose:
SUPER-CHARGER SPRINT SET
SUPER-CHARGER RALLY 'N FREEWAY SET
SUPER-CHARGER GRAND PRIX SET
SUPER-CHARGER RACE SET
ADJUSTABLE
Change comp
HOT WHEELS
3-D SHO
PLAQUES
The Custom
4 cars; the
holds 7. So
ing, they ma
their own.
Custom-Shop
We got the goods. You get the goodies.

Hot Wheels
FASTEST METAL CARS IN THE WORLD!
New from Mattel. The fastest miniature cars you've ever seen. And look at these features!
Exclusive torsion bar suspension that really works.
Customized engines.
Mag wheels. Red stripe slicks.
Pipes.
Detailed underbody.
All metal chassis and body.
Low friction wheel bearings for super speed.
Choose from 16 new California custom styled Hot Wheels!
Custom Mustang
Custom Cougar
Custom Camaro
Custom Corvette
Custom Barracuda
Custom Eldorado
Deora
Cheetah
MATTEL HOT WHEELS
Hot Wheels collector button comes with every car.
Custom Fleetside
Custom T-Bird
Custom El Dorado
Beatnik Bandit
Custom Firebird
Silhouette
Ford J-Car
Custom Volkswagen
Hot Heap
Get new Hot Wheels in action sets, too! With up to 30 feet of special track and accessories, so you can race 'em, or stunt 'em!

In 1969, Mattel came out with
24 more **models**. And by
1991, the company had built
its 1 billionth Hot Wheels car.

Hot Wheels cars remain extremely popular today. Mattel releases new **models** every year. Each one is just as cool and speedy as Elliot hoped!

More Facts

- Until 1977, Mattel had thin red lines painted around the sidewalls of Hot Wheels tires. Models with red on the tires sell for thousands of dollars today!

- Hot Wheels' white enamel Custom Camaro prototype is extremely rare. Today, the toy car is worth an estimated $100,000!

- Hot Wheels was inducted into the National Toy Hall of Fame in 2011.

Glossary

debuting – (of a product) launching or being seen by the public for the first time.

die-cast – made by die casting. Die casting is a process in which molten metal is poured into steel molds—also known as dies.

founded – set up and created.

inducted – brought in as a member.

luster – a gentle sheen or soft glow.

model – a small, exact copy of something; a type or design of a product.

prototype – a first or early model of something from which other forms are copied.

striking – causing a strong impression; very noticeable or remarkable.

Index

Visit **abdokids.com** to access crafts, games, videos, and more!